1

The Life and Times of

Tiffany Carpenter

By: Briana L Barnes

Dedication:

I dedicate this book to all of my supporters and everyone who believed

that I could do it. You mean more than you know.

PART ONE

I will start off a while back to the year 2000-2001. This is the year my life became a mess. This is where all the trouble started. So far, being Tiffany Carpenter wasn't the easiest any longer. This all came to be because of a guy (go figure, right?). I mean, what else is new? Boys are nothing but trouble.

His name was Tim. He was cute, funny, and my best friend. There was just one problem, my best friend for my whole life started liking him too. She was going to tell him.

"What am I going to do?" I thought to myself. "I should have told her a long time ago. Why didn't I? I have too." Maybe it's because she was gorgeous, and I was just me.

So I wrote her a note. Was it the coward's way out? Probably, but it was the only way I could get it out of me. I let everything out in that note and just as I suspected would happen, happened. Brittany didn't accept it. She avoided me for the rest of the day. It's moments like these that make me believe it is better to keep things to myself. Some secrets should never be told.

Later that night Brittany called me.
"Hey Tiff, I have to tell you something."

"If it's about you and Tim then I already know."

" How did you find out?"

"Emily told me, and you don't usually start off a conversation with 'Tiff I have to tell you something' unless you did something you knew would upset me."

"So you're mad I said yes?"

"Did you think I'd be happy after what I told you earlier?"

"Can you at least be happy for me?

"Fine."

-CLICK-

You read that right, they're together. I hung up the phone because I couldn't take it any longer. "Was I mad?" Of course I'm mad! Furious is more like it.

Why wouldn't I be angry? I couldn't talk to her. She hurt me. My emotions are raging. "I got it," I shouted. Everyone looked at me like I was nuts. It was probably because at this point I was in school in my Algebra class. Oh well. My pain can be expressed through other ways. I knew what I was going to do. I was going to bleed it out. "I can wear long shirts and no one will know. It's perfect!" I thought to myself.

Later that night I was going to do it. I had to do it. I mean you have to understand… My life is a mess. This will help me.

Just when I was about to make the cut, the phone rang.

"Hello?" I say.

"Tiff, it's Brittany. We need to talk."

" No, we really don't."

" Uh, yes we definitely do."

"About?"

"You know."

"I don't want to! Plus I am in the middle of doing something important."

"What could be so important?"

"Getting rid of my emotional pain!"

"By what?"

"Causing myself physical pain!"

"Tiff you can't!"

"Oh yeah?" I grabbed the razor and made the cut. "Mmm..." I sighed.

"You didn't!"

"Oh but I did. Maybe I wouldn't have felt so hurt and upset if you listened to me earlier, when I told you how I felt."

"What do you want me to do?"

"The right thing!"

"Break up with Tim?"

"It sure would make me feel better."

"Well I won't!"

-CLICK-

Once again I could not take her nonsense. I thought she understood. Her of all people. I hate her so much right now.

I can't explain it. The good thing is I feel better. The cut is deep but I am better. That's all that mattered. "I'll keep it covered, and I'll blame my cat." I thought to myself.

The only flaw to this plan is that Brittany knows and she'll tell everyone.

"UGH!" I screamed.

-RING, RING-

"Hello?" I said.

"Um, is this Tiff?"

"No it's the easter bunny!"

"Ha, Ha."

"Who is this anyway?"

"It's Tim. I really need to talk to you."

"Did she tell you?"

"Maybe."

"UGH! What did she say? I know it has something to do with the cut so spit it out."

"Why?"

"Why what? Be more specific. I can't read minds."

"Why did you cut yourself?"

"Why did you ask her out?"

"So that's what this is about? You're jealous of your friend because she got the man of your dreams?"

"Wait a minute. Back up the train, their buddy. Jealous? Me? No! Furious is more like it. She knew I liked you. You knew I liked you. But you two did it anyway. So much for best friends."

"Listen, if it makes you feel any better. We'll end it. We talked about it an hour ago and we feel it's what's right."

"That's because it is right! You know what? Do whatever the heck you two want. Why does it matter anyway? The damage is done!"

-CLICK-

I haven't ever hung up the phone so much in my life! They just weren't making sense. Plus, jealous? I don't think so. Angry definitely but I have the right to be.

The next day was crazy and weird. There was just so much tension between us at school. Brittany and Tim looked angry but oh so happy with each other. It drove me crazy. How could they do that to me? I really needed to get some better best friends. I have one who likes the guy I like and winds up going out with him. Then I have another one who likes my best friend and asks her out even though they both know how I feel. I had to talk to someone.

-DIAL TONE-

"Hi, is Emily there? It's Tiffany."

"This is Emily."

"Oh, hey. I didn't recognize your voice. You sound so different over the phone."

"Really? That's weird. So what are you calling me for? You hardly do. Is something wrong?"

"I am a horrible friend! Sorry I rarely call. It's just that when this year started trouble started. Can you say DRAMA."

"Drama, ha."

"Ha ha you're funny!"

"Tiff, is this about Brit and Tim?"

"Maybe."

"Okay, I'm listening. Spill."

"At least you listen. Anyway I'm so confused. How can I be happy for her when she knows? Plus, he knew! How can I forgive or forget this? Em, help!"

"Well I don't know what to say. It's complicated. It's wrong what she did but, it's also wrong what you're doing."

"What do you mean?"

"Well you shouldn't be ignoring them. You should tell them how you feel. Tiff, talk to them."

"They know how I feel. I told them before I hung up on them yesterday."

"Well I don't know what to say except try to work this out. You've been friends for so long."

"Yeah, I know but this is hard."

"I'll talk to her."

"Thanks Em, you're the best."

"I know, I know."

"You're funny!"

" Hey, I gotta go!"

"Okay, no problem."

"Bye."

"Later."

-CLICK-

She didn't help very much but, I guess it's a start. She said I was in the wrong too. "Am I?" I thought. "I can't be! I wouldn't have done this to her!" I had come to the realization that night. I had to become closer with people who are affected with this the same way that I am. I had to become closer to Michelle. I was going to, too.

The next day Brittany and Tim were ignoring me. I didn't care though. I may as well just stop liking guys for now and focus on what really matters: school and friendships.
Focusing is what I needed to do. Still, no matter how hard I tried; I couldn't get Tim off my mind. I hated it so much. Why does he consume my thoughts? He is with my best friend. I should be over it, over him already. I had to talk to them. So I swallowed my pride and I went over to them.

"Hey." I said.

"Uh, hi." Brittany replied.

"Yeah." Tim said.

"I really need to talk to you guys about how I feel about everything."

"Okay we're listening." Tim answered for both of them.

"Alright, I'm mad. I feel like I've been stabbed in the back. You both knew how I felt and you did it anyway. I feel betrayed. I'm just confused with everything."

"Tiff, I'm really sorry. I just couldn't resist." Brittany replied.

"I couldn't resist either." He leaned in and kissed her.

"I'm out of here! I knew talking to you guys wouldn't make a difference. BYE."

I left. How could they kiss and do that right in front of my face. When two people try to hurt people, they succeed. I went home that day and cried and cried. I couldn't get this off of my mind. I was going to cut myself to feel better but the phone rang in the nick of time.

-RING, RING-

"Hello?" I answer.

"Hey Tiff!"

" Who is this?"

"A concerned person."

"Who? Concerned about what?"

"I'm concerned about your feelings. I saw what happened today. I know how you feel about Tim and Brittany."

"Thanks but who is this?"

"It's Michelle."

"Oh, hey. I didn't know you were around when they kissed. How did you know?"

"You make it pretty obvious."

"I do?"

"Yeah."

"Well that's just wonderful."

"Listen, I want to tell you something."

"Okay, shoot. I'm listening."

"Alright, well I like Tim too."

"Really? So you kind of understand how I feel."

"Um, yeah. I do, at least a little bit. Though Brit is your best friend and she's just my friend. If I can even call her that. I mean I understand that you're hurt because I am too. You're more hurt then I am because she's closer to you. Do you understand what I'm trying to say?"

"Yeah. You're saying that you're hurt because you like him and you understand that I'm in a lot of pain because they're both my best friends. Now I have a question for you. Did she know you liked Tim?"

"No she doesn't know."

"Oh, well then I can understand."

"Why do you even bother with them anymore anyway?"

"Because I don't want to give up on my friends. I never have and I don't plan on starting now."

"You see, that's why I like having you as a friend. You care about your friends and you don't let them go no matter what."

"Thanks."

"You're welcome! Hey, my mom is calling me. I have to go. Bye."

"Bye."

-CLICK-

Wow! I wasn't even trying to get close with any other friends yet and they were trying to get close to me. This has never happened to me before. I'm usually the one who has to go and make the first move in these situations. It's nice to have someone that cares about me and my feelings. It's good to have someone who understands. For once what was going on in my life matters to someone. Michelle is a good friend, and I don't know why I didn't try and get closer with her before.

The next day at school I was actually happy. I spent the day avoiding Tim and Brittany which was a little hard because we were in all of the classes. I managed though. Michelle was a big help. We talked all day and I told her a lot of things she didn't know about me. She also told me a lot that I didn't know about her. It was a really good day. I couldn't believe how much fun I was having. I ruined it though, naturally. I had one minute of quiet time and it ruined everything. All the fun I was and how happy I was went away the minute I heard Tim and Brit flirting. Then, at that moment I realized how mad I was. I started shaking. That hasn't ever happened to me before. It was scary, but I could stop. It was like I was a puppet on a string and they controlled me.

"Are you okay?" Michelle asked.

"I don't know." I said.

"Why are you shaking?"

"I don't know, but I can't stop."

"Well what's wrong? You were just really happy. Then we got quiet for like a minute and you started shaking."

"I was having a good time for once. Then I heard them (pointing) flirting and all of the sudden BOOM! I start shaking and I realize how mad I am. Now I can't stop shaking."

"I'll be back. I need to take care of something really quick."

She walked away. I had no idea where or what she was going to do. Until:

"Brittany, I need to talk to you. In private if you don't mind." Michelle said.

"Um, okay?"

They walked into the hallway after Michelle told Mrs. Morales she had a personal question she had to ask Brittany in the hallway.

"What the heck is your problem?" Michelle practically screams.

"What are you talking about?"

"You are so stupid. I swear!"

"I'm lost."

"Well of course you are. Because you aren't smart. You're risking the best friendship you've ever had over a guy. Haven't you heard of chicks before dicks?"

"This is between Tim, me, and Tiff. Not you!"

"Whoa honey. Don't get an attitude with me. This is between me too. You want to know why? Because I am Tiff's best friend and I actually care about her feelings and her emotional health. She's in there shaking and she can't stop. All because she is very angry about this whole situation."

"She's shaking?"

"Yeah, but I'm pretty sure you don't care anyway."

"Yes, I do."

"I know you are lying. You care about Tim a lot more than Tiff. You know what? You need to fix this, or I will."

Michelle walked back into the classroom steamed. She looked so mad. I had never seen her like this. So red in the face. She looked like she was going to hit someone. I decided I wasn't going to ask until later what happened.

Eventually, I asked her. She was in better spirits. She was laughing so I figured it was the perfect time. She told me everything and I was never happier to have a friend like her, someone to stick up for me when worse came to worst. Michelle had definitely become a part of me.

I was definitely happy now. I had a good friend. Yet, I was sad. The whole thing with Brittany and Tim was still affecting me. I just wanted it to be over already. I was really sick of the pain this was causing. I was also still a little shaky. I wasn't going to cut myself again because it really wasn't the smartest thing to do. I was bored and getting antsy. I watched tv for a while, and the phone rang.

-RING,RING-

"Hello?" I said.

"Hey, it's Michelle! What are you doing?"

"Oh, nothing. I was just watching some Tv. There was nothing really good on though."

"That's cool. I'm really bored too. There is nothing to do."

"Hey, I wanted to say thanks."

"For what?"

"For talking to Brittany. No one has ever done anything like that for me."

"Well, you're my best friend. Also, no one deserves to be treated the way they are treating you."

"Thanks for understanding too."

"It's really nothing. I mean you're a good friend and I want to help you because you helped me."

"How did I help you?

"You talked to me. Before you no one really understood me at all. Or bothered to talk to me. So when you were having this problem, I jumped on the chance to help you out."

-BEEP, BEEP-

"Hey Michelle can you hold on a moment. My other line is beeping."

"Sure, no problem."

-CLICKS OVER-

"Hello? Tiffany speaking, how may I help you?"

"It's Brittany!"

"Oh, what do you want?"

"I want to apologize."

"Can you hold on? Someone is on the other line."

"Sure."

-CLICKS BACK OVER-

"Oh my gosh Michelle, it's Brit what should I do?"

"Well, what does she want?"

"She wants to apologize."

"Well, listen to her and see what she says. I'll be waiting! Tell me everything!"

"Okay."

-CLICKS BACK OVER-

"Brit?"

"I'm still here."

"Um, you were saying?"

"Oh yeah. I'm sorry Tiff. Tim and I broke up today. We decided that our friendship with you is more important. We hope you can forgive us."

"You broke up? For me?"

"Yeah Tiff. We miss you. We miss talking to you."

"Okay. I forgive you."

"Really?"

"Yeah. I have to go. I'll see you in school tomorrow."

"Okay, Bye."

-CLICKS OVER-

"Michelle?"

"Yeah?"

"They broke up!"

"Really? I bet you're happy!"

"I am! They said they did it for me because they miss me."

"Hold on, I'm marking this down in my calendar. December 30,2000. Brit and Tim break up for unselfish reasons."

"You're such a drama queen."

"I know but that's why you love me."

"Yeah, yeah."

"Hey, I have to go."

"No problem! Later!"

"Bye!"

-CLICK-

So they broke up. I was happy. Maybe things were finally taking a turn for the better. Who knows? Let's see how long it will last this time. It seems too good to be true. But I will deal with it.

The next day rolled around. It went pretty smoothly. Me, Brit, and Tim were all talking again as if nothing was wrong. Even though to me there was. I mean sure I was glad we were friends again and all but there was so much tension. And even though I could see they were trying they really couldn't they really couldn't help but flirt. It hurt a lot.

Later that day Michelle came over and I couldn't keep it in any longer.

"I don't like this," I said.

"What are you talking about?"

"Brit and Tim."

"What about them?"

"They still rub it in my face."

"How? I thought they were done?"

"I know. So did I, but still he's always touching her thighs and they flirt so much. It hurts like…UGH!"

"Calm down Tiff. I understand what you're going through."

"I shouldn't have trusted them. I made a huge mistake once again."

"Don't tell me you're going to go all emo on me."

"What do you mean?"

"I know you cut yourself Tiff. I'm not stupid. I'm your best friend. Did you seriously think I wouldn't find out sooner or later? You couldn't keep it a secret forever."

"And you still want to be my friend?"

"Of course, I get it. It isn't right to do but I understand. You don't need to do it. I'm here for you."

"Thanks! I know it's wrong but I can't help it sometimes."

"It's okay, now let's get back to our project."

We worked until about nine p.m. It was a long day. Then we ate and Michelle wound up spending the night. The next morning my mother took her home.

"Tiff, sweetie, let's go visit your grandmother," my mother yelled up the stairs.

"Okay! How long are we going to be gone?"

"A while, we are going to the Patterson's!"

"Who? Why?"

"The Patterson's. They go to our meetings. They invited us over."

"Ugh! Fine!"

"Be nice."

PART TWO

I didn't remember the Patterson's. I proceeded to get dressed. I didn't care what I looked like. I mean I don't even know who they were. I threw on baggy sweatpants and a Brooklyn T-Shirt and a black hoodie. I put my hair up in a messy bun and was finished.

-PHONE RINGS-

"Hello," I answered.

"You answered the phone quickly."

"That's the advantage of having your own phone."

"Such an attitude. Do you know who this is?"

"Nope."

"It's your father. I live in New York now with Betsy."

"Well, hello dad. Who is Betsy? What happened to Teresa?

"Things didn't work out."

"So how long have you been with Betsy? The last time I talked to you was three months after you left seven years ago."

"Sorry."

"You should be, you're lucky I even forgave you."

"For?"

"Um, maybe the black and blues, the scars, uh everything. Abusive words. I could go in if you'd like."

"Sorry again. I actually called to ask you something. Can you, no, do you want to come visit me in New York with your brother?"

"What about the twins?"

"Them too."

"For what?"

"My wedding."

"I'll ask. Listen, I have to go. We're going to be leaving."

"Okay, love ya."

"Bye Dad."

-CLICK-

That was horrible. I can't believe he called me. My parents didn't work out. They had me right away and they struggled. Then came my brother and then the twins.
I was nine, Virg was five, and the twins were two when he left with no reason. I was relieved though because he took out his anger on me after he and my mom would fight. Especially on the day she

kicked him out. I thought it was my fault. My mom then filed for divorce and since my dad hit us (especially me) my mom won custody.

He was cheating on my mom the whole time. Right after the twins were born he started. It was with Teresa the whore. She knew he was married. She even knew he had kids. She didn't care. I hate her.

-PHONE RINGS-

"Hello?" I said very hastily.

"Wow."

"Who is this?"

"James."

"Oh my gosh! How are you? Where have you been? It's been so long!"

"I know. I moved. I missed everyone. Especially you."

"You moved? Wow. I am so out of the loop. I missed you too."

"I'm coming back, I'll be going to UCG Tech."

"That's where I go!"

"Really? The team is going to be back together again."

"I know."

"Hey, do you remember four years ago when.."

"We went out for three months?" I interrupted.

"How did you know I was going to say that?

"Because I know you."

"Too well. What am I going to say now?"

"I don't know. Surprise me."

"Do you want to try us again?"

"Well if you're coming back then why not?"

"Cool. Well I am going to be back by Monday."

"That's two days."

"I know."

"Wow. Hey, I have to go. Grandma awaits."

"Later lover."

"You're funny.

(Share laughs)

"Bye."

-CLICK-

I walked down the steps and went into the kitchen where my mom was.

"I hope this is okay for the Patterson's mom. Who are they anyway?" I asked.

"You'll see after grandma's. You look fine."

"You'll never guess who just called."

"Who?"

"Well two people did."

"Who and who?"

"Dad and---"

"Your father called?" She asked, cutting me off.

"Yeah."

"What did he want?"

"To talk."

"And?"

"And invite me, Virg, and the twins to New York."

"Why?"

"For his wedding."

"He's marrying Teresa?"

"No. Betsy."

"Who?"

"That's what I said."

"Well, do you want to go?"

"I don't care."

"You can."

"Then I will. I'll wear black a very nice fancy black dress and like I'm at a funeral because as soon as they say I do, it's over."

"Now I'm definitely letting you go."

"Good."

"Who else called?"

"James."

"The former flame?"

"And current."

"But he's gone."

"Not anymore, he's back."

"OOOOH," she teased.

"Shut up mom!"

"Go get your brothers and sister."

"Okay."

I walked away. I went to the bottom of the stairs and shouted: "Virg?"

"What do you want, Tiff?

"Come downstairs. We're leaving."

"Where are we going?"

"Grandma's then the Patterson's."

"Who?"

"That's what I said!

"I'm coming!"

Then I turned around, turned the corner, and walked down the hall to the twins room and knocked on the door.

"Hey terrible two!" I screamed.

(Door opens and it's Ann-Marie)

"What do you want?" She asks.

"Get Gregy, we're leaving."

"To Grandma's?" he shouts from the back of the room.

"Uh-huh. You better hurry."

Greg ran past me in a hurry. Ann-Marie ran after him shouting, "Wait for me!" He didn't listen. Greg loves his Grandma, and so do I. Sometimes she is the only one who understands.

We all threw on our coats and hopped in the van. On our way to Grandma's we went. It takes about thirty minutes to get to her house. I sat in the front. Virg sat all the way in the back. That leaves the twins in the middle.

We arrived at Grandma's house at about 2:30 PM. We did the basic things. We went to eat, and hung out at her house. Then my mom told her we had plans and off we went.

So now we were on our way to the Patterson's. I spent the whole day thinking about James and trying to remember or even realize who the Patterson's were. I drew a complete blank.

Thinking about James was fun though. I mean he's just so cute and he's my friend, and he knows me so well. We get along. The team is back together again. I couldn't have had a better day. So far I mean.

We pulled up next to a house I didn't recognize.

"Uh, where are we?" I asked my mom.

"Here."

"Where is here exactly?"

"The Patterson's."

"Oh yeah, I forgot."

"Stop thinking about James, and get out of the car."

"You think you're so funny."

"I don't think, I know."

We got out of the car. I looked around and didn't recognize where I was. We all walked to the door and I got to ring the doorbell.

They got to the door quickly. We were greeted by a boy my age. I've seen him around. I recognized him. I just couldn't remember his name. I felt a little bad about it though.

There was something about him, he was cute. I could tell he was thinking the same thing about me when I saw how he was looking at me. Then as he was walking over to me, it hit me. He goes to my school.

"Don't you go to UCG Tech?" We both asked.

"Yes, I do." We both replied.

We laughed.

"My name is Tiffany. And you are?"

"Dante."

"Oh, okay."

"I think we're supposed to be over there."

"Yeah, let's go. So any girlfriends?"

"Well as a matter of fact, yes. How about you, any boy friends?"

"Yeah, his name is James."

"That's cool. My girl's name is Keana."

"Does she go to our school?"

"Yeah, how about James?"

"He will be starting Monday. You see he moved and we used to date but we had to end it due to the fact that, well I don't really want to talk about it."

"It's okay."

"So how long have you been with Keana?"

"A month."

"So you're just starting out?"

"Yeah."

"Do you really like her?"

"Well, I like her."

"I get it, you're confused."

"Yeah."

"Starting to like someone else?"

"As of now, yeah."

"Me too."

"So Tiff?"

"Yeah?"

"Do you have a cellphone?"

"But of course."

"Ha. Ha. What is your number?"

"484-179-3268."

"Cool mine is 484-975-2345."

"Now we should probably go in there with them."

"I agree."

We joined the rest of the group as you can call it. It's ironic both of our parents are single. I think they are going to be real close. Maybe me and Dante would be too. As friends I mean. I have James and he has Keana.

Even though I know that I couldn't help but feel a connection with this guy. I was starting to think I liked him and I had a feeling he liked me too.

I spent the whole night confused. I couldn't like someone else. I have a boyfriend. I just don't know anymore. We were there for 5 hours. We didn't leave until one o'clock in the morning.

The drive home was quiet. Well up until my mom opened her mouth.

"So Tiff."

"What mom?"

"You were getting pretty close with Dante."

"Yeah. He's cool. He's nice too."

"So you're friends?"

"Yup."

"That's good!"

"I know."

"What about you guys?"

"I had fun," Virgil said.

"Good, good. And you guys?" Mom asked again.

"We like Stephy," The twins said.

Dante was my age. I was right. Virgil had a companion too. His name is Kevin. The twins did too, Stephy. Looks like there was someone for everyone.

We went home and I went to my room. I had to call Michelle. My day was crazy and she could help me shuffle through my head. She's good at that. So I picked up the phone and dialed her number.

-RING-

"Hello?"

"Hey it's me Tiff!"

"What's up?"

"I had the craziest day!"

"I'm listening."

"Well first off, my dad called."

"The dead beat?"

"Mmhmm."

"What did he want?"

"To invite me, Virgil, and the Twins to New York to go to his wedding."

"Do you want to go?"

"I don't even know anymore."

"Well what else happened?"

"James."

"That guy you were totally in love with?"

"Yeah."

"What about him?"

"We're back together again."

"Oh really?"

"Yeah."

"Well what else happened? It sounds like there is more."

"I met this guy."

"Uh-oh."

"No, he's just a friend. I think."

"You think?"

"I don't know. We got along, and he is very nice, plus he's cute. But he has a girlfriend."

"And you have a boyfriend."

"Yeah I guess. Hey, someone is texting me. I gotta go."

"Later!"

We hung up. My phone was vibrating in my pocket. I took it out to see who it was. It was Dante. I didn't know whether or not to reply to his message. He wrote, "Hi. What's up?" I guess it wouldn't hurt to talk to him.

"Nothing much," I said.

"I'm really bored. How's your boyfriend?

"I don't know. He hasn't called."

"Oh."

"How's Keana?"

"Good."

"Alright. I'm going to go."

"Why?"

"I'm tired. It's two in the morning."

"Alright. Bye."

"Later."

That was odd. I can't believe he texted me. This late, too. I didn't care though. That was just it though, I should have cared.

The next day I did nothing. I talked on the phone, and watched T.V., and I thought. I really wanted to go to school tomorrow. I wanted to see James because it has been so long since I 've seen him. Plus, I wanted to see Dante and meet Keana.

I kept thinking over our conversation. He said "as of now yeah" about liking someone. Could that mean he liked me? I mean he texted me at two o'clock in the morning to ask me about my boyfriend. Maybe I'm blowing this whole thing out of proportion.

It was late. I was happy. That meant it was almost time for school. I had a problem though. Who was I more excited to see? Dante or James? I went to sleep on that thought.

It was morning now. I had to look good. I wanted to look good. So I went to my closet. "What to wear? What to wear?" I said aloud.

I found my outfit. I was wearing my black fishnet top and my black jeans. The ones with the holes. I was ready to go.

I arrived at school and met up with Michelle, then we went to breakfast. There I met up with James. I ran over to him and gave him the biggest hug ever. Then he kissed me. It was then that I realized how much I had really missed him. He pulled away just for me to kiss him again. Then I saw Dante. He was kissing his girlfriend. I was kind of angry about it. But it was okay.

They came over to us, Dante and Keana.

"Hey Tiff," Dante said.

"Hey," I said with a smile.

"This is Keana."

"Hi," I said to her.

She said nothing. She just looked at James with a smile on her face. He was smiling back at her. That made me mad.

"This is James," I said to them.

"Hi!" Keana said in this excited, flirty voice.

Dante and I shared looks. He signaled me over to him. I went with no hesitations. We left James and Keana. Not knowing then what was going to happen. He wanted to talk.

"So what do you make of that?" He said.

"I don't know, they're really hitting it off."

"Jealous?"

"Are you?"

"Maybe."

"Same here."

"I don't get it."

"What don't you get?"

"I don't get why I can't find a decent girl. You know? Like a friend, kind of, someone who understands and won't hurt me. You know?"

"I completely understand."

"Look at them."

"What are they doing?"

"What do you think that paper says?"

"Probably exchanging digits."

"I bet you're right."

"I know I am."

"Confident?"

"Very."

"Bet they'll lie about it."

"I have no doubts."

They came over to us. Dante hugged me goodbye, and then Keana grabbed his hand and they walked away. Then James grabbed mine and gave me a kiss. But that wasn't going to make me forget about him and Keana. I had to figure out what that paper said.

"What was that?" I asked.

"What do you mean?" James said.

"You know what I mean! What did that paper say?"

"There is no paper."

"LIAR!"

"Okay, okay."

"What did it say?"

"Relax. She just gave me her number."

"And you gave her yours. Do you like her?"

"What? No! What about that Dante kid? You two were awfully close."

"Chill. Our parents are friends. We're just friends."

"You're overreacting."

"I am not!"

"Can we just drop this?"

"Fine."

"I'm sorry!"

"Whatever."

He kissed my cheek. Then he walked away. I wasn't so sure about this. It was his first day back, he's with me, and now there's someone trying to take him away.

It was a new semester. That means new classes. James, Keana, and Dante were in my first period class. Then all the others only Dante was in. It was kind of awkward. It was only later that I found out that Keana was in the rest of James' classes. Nothing good could come of this.

The next day was weird. Since everyone needed to get used to their new classmates, we had the whole day off.

First period was different. Not in a good way. We made our little group. It was James, Keana, Dante, and me.

"So how long have you and Tiff known each other? Keana asked James.

"Since we were seven," he said.

"Wow, that's a really long time. You guys must be close," she said sadly.

"Yeah, she's an amazing friend."

"Friend! That's it! I have had enough of this! I am out of here!" I shouted.

I got up and left the classroom. The teacher could tell I was angry so she had no problem with it. Dante followed me out. He pulled me into him and hugged me.

"Are you okay?" he asked.

"I can't believe them. He is such a jerk. He said he loved me. Yeah right! He's too busy flirting with that stuck up little hooker Keana to remember that I'm his girlfriend!"

"Wow, you're really angry. And you're right about Keana. She is a … never mind."

"I'm ending it."

"Really?"

"Yeah, I'm done."

"Oh… okay."

"Are you coming?"

"Oh, yeah."

We walked to the door. That's when it happened. That's when we saw it. Them, James and Keana. MAKING OUT. Me and Dante were so mad. We opened the door, walked in, and sat down. They didn't even notice us. What's worse is the teacher didn't even care. It went on for like fifteen minutes. It was like no one was around. I finally got sick of it.

"Excuse me!" I screamed.

They pulled away.

"Uh-Oh." They said.

"How long has this been going on? I said.

"Not long." Keana said.

"I wasn't talking to you, you little whore."

"Excuse me?"

"You heard me, what are you going to do about it?"

"This."

She punched me. That is when everything broke loose. I guess I was so mad I unleashed everything on her. She didn't look that bad when I was finished.

"Young lady!" The teacher screamed.

"Oh, so now you pay attention. To what do we owe this honor?

"That is enough."

"UGH!"

"Stop raising your voice to me!"

"NO!"

He walked away. Everyone gave me that look. Like they didn't know I had it in me. The teacher called me over and gave me a paper. I was sent to the disciplinary office. Why do I get myself into these situations? I waited for my turn to get my sentencing. That's what I'm calling it.

When I was done with them I wound up with two days of out of school suspension. Really hard punishers. Now I had to deal with my mother.

I got sent home early. My mom wasn't home from work yet. So I decided that I would walk to the Twins school and meet her there. So I did and I found my mom.

"Hey." I said.

"Why aren't you in school?"

"About that."

"What happened?"

"This."

I pulled out the paper with my write up on it, and I handed it over. I watched her as she read it. She went from happy to serious and then concerned.

"Wow. Why?" She asked.

"Because the hooker hit me first. But of course I get all the blame because I did all of the damage."

"Anger issues."

"Yes."

"Why though?"

"James."

"Why did you even fall for him again after he hurt you like that the last time?"

"I'm stupid."

"No, you're not."

"Sh! Here come the Twins."

"Tiff!" They screamed, and hugged me.

"Hey, terrible two."

We went home. My mom kind of left me alone. I guess she knew I needed to blow off steam. We ate dinner and still nothing. Then it got late so I got ready for bed.
I woke up to find my dad in the living room.

"To what do I owe this honor?" I asked.

"Go and pack your bags. You're coming with me."

"Why?"

"To visit. I talked to your mom. She's fine with it and it's not like you're going anywhere."

"But what about Virgil? Ann-Marie? Greg? They're supposed to come too."

"No. They're not."

"But your wedding?"

"Not for three more months. Now quit hassling me and go pack."

"Chill out! I'm going! How long should I pack for?

"The weekend."

So now I'm going with my father? And I thought it couldn't get any worse. Oh well. How bad could it be? I packed my pjs and clothes. Maybe this will be okay. I need to get away.

I went downstairs with my backpack.

"Ready?" My dad asked.

"Yeah, but I'm hungry."

"We'll pick something up on the way."

So I got into his car. It was nice but not very spacious. One of those new expensive cars. Obviously, he was doing very well. There is such an awkward silence in the car with him. I feel so weird around him. Especially because of what he used to do to me. One does not forget the beating.

"Excited to meet Betsy?" He said.

"No, not really. I'm going to have a stepmom."

"Be nice!"

"I'll think about it."

-Ring, Ring-

"Hello?" I said.

"Hey hunny, are you with your dad?"

"Mom?"

"Yes, dear."

"Why?"

"He's concerned and so am I."

"Is he going to take me somewhere?"

"No. You're just getting away."

"Whatever. I gotta go."

"Bye."

-CLICK-

"Was that your mother?" Dad asked.

"No, it was Morgan Freeman."

"I'm tired of your attitude."

"And I'm tired of your abandonment, then coming back assuming that everything will be okay. Do me a favor, keep your eyes on the road and don't talk to me."

He pulled over. I feared the worst. I was right, again. He started hitting me. As if I didn't get enough of that when I was a kid. I kept quiet. I let him drive while I texted. I was pissed. I told my mom everything. She was angry. He wasn't supposed to do that. That was their deal. She's going to press charges. I have bruises and I took pictures of them. He isn't going to get away with this. Not again!

I pulled out my phone again. I wanted to text Dante.

"Hello." I typed.

"How is your time off?"

"Not so good."

"Why? What happened?"

"My dad."

"What about him?"

"He picked me up."

"For?"

"Some plan he and my mom made."

"Which would be?"

"I have no idea."

"Anything else?"

"He beat me."

"Oh my gosh!"

"Yeah, again… just like old times."

"Are you okay?"

"I'll be fine."

"Good."

"Enough about me. What's up?"

"I've been thinking."

"About?"

"You."

"What about me?"

"How I can't get you off of my mind."

"Really?"

"Yeah, I can't stop thinking about you. Not since the day we met."

"Me either."

"Are you serious?"

"Uh… yeah. I wouldn't have said it if I wasn't."

"Cool."

"So, did you hear?"

"What?"

"James and Keana are dating."

"Oh yeah, they belong together."

"Seriously."

"I have to ask you something."

"Then ask already."

"Will you go out with me?"

"Yes, I will. I thought you'd never ask."

"Cool."

"Wow. What a week."

"I know. You're telling me."

"Hey, I gotta go. We're in New York now. I'll call you later."

"Okay."

The city of lights. The city that never sleeps. We finally arrived. My dad's house is huge. A penthouse apartment. I was prepared to meet my future stepmom. My dad lived on the twenty fifth floor.

When we got to the door I became nervous. I mean why did I have to come here by myself? What was my parents' plan? Secrets. I hate them.

He opened the door. I was amazed at the cleanliness, the space.

"Betsy do all of the cleaning around here?" I said with a laugh.

"Why yes she does. Why?"

"Great, a clean freak. Visiting you should be a blast."

"What did I say about that attitude?"

"Sorry!"

"That's better."

"So why am I here?"

"To visit."

"Ugh! Where is my room?"

"Follow me."

I did. Down the hall fourth door on the left. It was bigger than my room at home. Three times the size.

"Dinner is at seven." My dad said.

"Got a phone around here?"

"Yeah it's on your nightstand."

"Thanks."

So I was stuck. Maybe I'll go out tonight. I mean it's New York. I want Dante to come up here. I want to see the Statue of Liberty. I also want to know why I am here. I guess I'll find out soon. I wanted to talk to my mom. I decided to call her.

-Dial Tone-

"Hello?" She said.

"Hey mom."

"How are your bruises?"

"Sore."

"What are you calling for?"

"Well I have news, and a question."

"Well, what's the question first?"

"Why am I here?"

"You'll find out tomorrow."

"UGH! Fine!"

"So is the news good or bad?"

"Super excellently fabulous."

"That good huh?"

"Yes!"

"So do you plan on telling me?"

"Dante is my boyfriend now."

"I knew this would happen! As of when?"

"Today."

"You go girl. Move on from that manwhore."

"Ha Ha! But I am happy now."

"That is all I want."

"Well I am going to go."

"Alright, call later."

"I promise."

-CLICK-

I knew my mom would accept the whole Dante thing. All she really cares about is my happiness. That's the difference between my mom and dad. My mom cares. My dad, well, he doesn't.

There was nothing for me to do. A couple of hours had passed when I got a text message.

"Hey." It read. It was from Dante.

"Hi." I typed back.

"Where are you in New York?"

"Brooklyn, why?"

"What is the address?"

"Gates Ave. The penthouse apartments."

"Alright."

"Why?"

"Come outside."

"Okay."

I grabbed my jacket. I told my dad I was leaving and hopped on the elevator. I thought the whole way down. Twenty five floors of thought. I wanted to know why I was going outside.

I reached the ground floor. I walked through the lobby and headed out the front door. I pulled out my phone.

"Now what?" I typed to Dante.

"Turn around."

I did and there he was. I couldn't believe my eyes. I hugged him. I felt such a rush with his embrace. I never felt that before, it was odd.

"What are you doing here?" I said.

"I wanted to see you."

"So you came all the way to New York? How did you get here?"

"I drove."

"For me?'

"Yeah."

"How sweet."

"I also came to do something else."

"What's that?"

"This."

His lips met mine. I felt a spark. I got so weak in my knees. I had to hold on to him.

"Wow." He said.

"What?"

"Oh, nothing."

"No, tell me."

"You're a really good kisser."

"You're not so bad yourself."

"Oh really?"

"Yeah, don't flatter yourself though."

"Hey!"

"I'm kidding."

"Oh yeah?"

"Yeah."

Then it happened again. We were kissing. My head emptied. I felt like no one else was around but him. I was falling. Faster than with any of the others.
With James, he was a mistake. I was blinded with love. But it wasn't really love. It was more of a friendship thing. Lust even.

With the others, I said I love you but it was puppy love. Not the real thing.
Dante is different though. There's just something about him. Could it be the oh so real spark I feel when we kiss? Or how I get butterflies just thinking about him? Or maybe it's the fact that my heart skips a beat when I lay my eyes on him? I don't know what it is but I don't love him yet. Or maybe I do. For now I'll just be confused.

Dante decided it would be nice to take me out to eat. So we wound up going to TGI Fridays. We had fun. We laughed and talked the whole time. We spent over two hours there. We left around 7:30PM.

After dinner we went on a carriage ride through Central Park. The stars (what we could see of them) were beautiful.
Then to top it all off he took me to the Statue of Liberty. We took a fairy boat there. We walked all the way up as far as we could go. The view was spectacular. Immaculate. The lights, the water, EVERYTHING. But what made it the most special was being there with him. Plus, the fact that it was all his idea was just so thoughtful.
He grabbed my hand. My stomach flip-flopped. But I didn't care.
He walked me home. Then he took me all the way to the twenty-fifth floor.

"So what are you going to do now?" I asked.

"Maybe I'll go stay at Holiday Inn or something. It's a little late for me to go all the way back home."

"Then why don't you stay here for the night?"

"I don't know."

"You won't have to waste any more of your money."

"Well okay then."

I grabbed his hand and then we walked through the hallway to the door. I grabbed the key and I led him in.

"Dad!" I shouted. There was no answer.

"I wonder where they are." I said.

"Maybe they went clubbing or drinking."

"My dad at a club? That's funny. But they might be drinking. I haven't even met Betsy yet."

"Well, why don't you call your dad?"

"Alright, I will be right back. Make yourself comfortable."

So I went into my room. I grabbed the phone and wondered where they were at.

-Dial Tone-

"Hello?" My dad said.

"Hey where are you?"

"At the bar."

"Where is Betsy?"

"With me."

"Oh okay. I have a favor."

"What?"

"Can a friend stay the night?"

"Who?"

"Dante."

"Sure, but I don't want any games."

"I know dad."

"Bye."

Well at least Dante could stay. I wasn't looking forward to the fact that my dad might be coming home drunk. Maybe he wouldn't do anything with Dante here though.
I walked into the living room. Dante was on the couch, relaxing.

"You were right." I said.

"About?"

"Drinking."

"I'm good like that."

"They said it's okay for you to stay."

"Alright."

"What do you want to do?"

"Doesn't matter."

"We could watch a movie."

"Which one?"

"It's a surprise."

I went to the cabinet. What to watch? There was such a huge collection to choose from. Knowing me I went for the gory one. Some movie about monsters taking over the world and killing off all humanity. Yeah, I'm into that stuff. I'm not like a lot of girls.
I popped the DVD in the player. Dante was surprised.

"You wanted to watch this?" Dante said jokingly.

"Yeah, it's my favorite movie."

"Wow."

"Wow what?"

"You're not what I expected, Tiffany. You're really not like anyone else."

"That is the wonder of Moi."

"Yeah."

"Sh! This is my favorite part."

He laughed at me. This was the part where they bomb the city. You know, Boom, Destruction.

I glanced up at Dante in a way where he wouldn't know I was looking at him. He was looking at me. I kept glancing up at him and every time I did, he was watching me.
I poked him.

"Hey, I have to ask you a question." I said.

"What?"
"Why are you looking at me? You're not even paying attention to the movie."

"No reason."

"Okay then."

"Tiffany?"

"Wh-"

I didn't get the chance to finish. He started kissing me. I hated the fact that he did that because every time he does I can't think straight.

He pulled away. Just in time too. My dad and Betsy walked through the door drunk and acting stupid.

Betsy was gorgeous. I hated it! But my mom is way prettier. He will never do as good as my mom ever again. Betsy tried talking to me but I just blew her off. I don't need to talk to her. My dad was mad at the fact that I couldn't even say hello.

"Tiffany Marie Carpenter!" He said.

"What?"

"Follow me."

I did. What is the worst that could happen?

"Why can't you be a nice young lady?" He asked.

"What are you talking about?"

"You don't even know how to say hi?"

"I am not going to speak to that whore."

He took off his belt and hit me. Then he smacked me across the mouth.

"What's your problem dad?" I said tears falling down my face.

"I have no problem! You're the one with the problem. But it will all be taken care of tomorrow when I send you to JKR's Mental Institution."

He was still hitting me. While beating me he said, "I hope they hurt you. I hope they mess you up really good."

"I hate you!"

I burst into tears. He kept on hitting me. And what could I do? I had to sit there and take it. It's no wonder I have so many problems. Who wouldn't be with him as a father?

He was finally finished. I went into my room and went into my bathroom to see the damage he did.

I had a huge black and blue on the side of my face.

I had a black eye and a scratch from my forehead to my mid-cheek. That belt, oh how I hate that belt. I couldn't go out to Dante looking like this.
What was I going to do? I put makeup on it. You could hardly tell anything was wrong. I walked back into the living room. Dante was sitting on the couch waiting for me.

I sat down next to him and he started stroking my cheek.

"Ow!" I screamed in pain.

"What's wrong?"

"Please, just don't touch my face."

"Why?"

"I'd rather not talk about it."

"Did he hit you again?"

I didn't answer. I just looked away.

"Tiffany, did he hit you again?"

I stayed quiet. Dante got up and went into the kitchen and turned the water on. He came back with a wet towel and wiped the side of my face. I clenched my teeth in pain.

"Oh my." He said.

He got really quiet. He pulled me close and held me. We sat in silence for an hour. Until he finally spoke.

"Did your dad always do this to you?"

"Yes. That's why my mom divorced him. They're sending me to a mental hospital. Here in New York. They think I'm nuts ever since I fought Keana. It's a good thing I'm suspended."

"What?"

"Yeah."

"That's messed up. But you do have some problems babe. Like your father for example."

"Yeah, I just hope I'm there for only one or two nights."

"Me too."

"Listen, I am in pain and I want to go to sleep. So."

"Go ahead. I'll see you in the morning."

I kissed him and went into my room. I couldn't even lay on the left side of my face. It hurt too badly. I had bruises on my chest, stomach, and arms. I had to call my mom. She needed to know. However, it was 4AM. So I let it wait. For now sleep is what I need and it overcame me.

When I woke up it was 9AM. My alarm clock went off. I didn't even set it. It was weird. I got dressed and put makeup on my bruise. I was just about to leave my room when I noticed something on my dresser. I picked it up. It was a letter from Dante. It said:

Dear Tiffany,
It is about five in the morning. Your dad just told me to get out of the house. So I have to hurry up. Call me when you get out of the mental hospital. You're not crazy, just misunderstood. They shouldn't keep you for long. I love you!
Love, Dante

I can't believe my father made him leave. What did he do? Nothing. He just did it to get to me. It worked.

I walked out to the kitchen where I saw my father at the table eating and reading the paper. Betsy was cooking.

"So." I said breaking the silence.

"What do you want?" My dad snapped back.

"What's for breakfast?"

"Food. Now shut up and sit down."

"Okay."

I sat down and Betsy brought me my breakfast. Bacon, eggs, and toast.

"When you're done eating, pack up your crap. You have an appointment at JKR. Or did you forget?" He said.

"I remember."

So I ate. Then I packed and waited in the living room. My appointment was at 11:00. That means I was leaving soon.

"Get off the couch, we're going. Come on. I don't have all day." My dad said.

"Okay."

We walked out. I didn't want to go. I am not crazy. I am misunderstood. The elevator down and the drive there went too fast. Too fast.

As soon as I stepped in I felt completely insane. People go here trying to commit suicide of trying to run their boyfriends over. I'm here because my mom and dad just think I'm crazy. They talked to me in private. I told them everything. How my father beat me. How I cut myself. The whole story. Then they called in my father. That's when they told us the news.

I have to stay for one week. One week of meetings with therapists and psychotherapists (as I call them). Talking about my problems. Then I can leave.

PART THREE

Time for a play by play.

DAY ONE:

Woke up. Ate breakfast that tasted like prison food. Disgusting. But hey what do you expect from a place like this? At least I don't have to share my room. I miss school. Anyway, back to my day of "fun." I had an appointment with Doctor Lopaski at 10:45 AM. Boy was that a wonderful experience. I was placed in some sort of machine that went around my head to check out my brain waves. If anything was wrong with me I would know by 4:30 PM. Next appointment was at 1:00 PM but this one was just a sit down session. Talking about my life, my family, my friends, the whole nine yards. Her name is Doctor Opitzki.

"Why hello there Tiffany." She said.

"Uh hi." I said back.

"For the next two hours you and I are going to talk."

"What could we possibly talk about?"

"You of course."

"Wonderful."

"So do you know why you're here dear?"

"Uh, no."

"You're here because you have an unstable emotional problem."

"Okay."

"Answer me this, sweetie, why do you cut yourself?"

"Because."

"That is not an answer."

"Yeah it is!"

"Listen, you can tell me anything. Everything you say is strictly confidential."

"I did it because there was a lot of crap going on and I couldn't take it anymore."

"I see. Have you ever thought about killing yourself?"

"Who hasn't? I mean everyone has those moments where nothing goes right and for that one second they just want to end it all. But my moments don't last for just a second. They last and last and last."

"I see. So then what's keeping you alive?"

"I don't know. I feel like I need to be around for my mom because ever since the divorce she's been falling apart. Also, I stay alive for my best friend. But then things happen that make me wonder if I'm stupid for wanting to stay alive. My dad beating me doesn't help."

"How often does your father beat you?"

"Well, since my mom won custody I don't really have to see him a lot. But there are those visits that I have to go to because I have no say in the matter. But whenever I do see him, he beats me. It's the worst when he is drunk because that's when the belt comes out."

"Did he hit you recently?"

"Yeah."

"When?"

"The night before I was admitted here."

"But that was yesterday."

"Yup."

"Did he leave any marks?"

"Yup."

"Where?"

"Where the damage was done."

I think something on my face gave it away because she threw water on my face and there went the makeup.

"Oh my." She stuttered.

"What it's like you haven't seen worse?"

"Not in all my days."

"Well now don't I feel special."

"Were there any other times since then? Well a little before that happened?"

"Yeah, that's when I got these." I lifted my shirt and showed the bruises on my chest, stomach, and back.

"My god!" She shouted.

"And there you go again."

"Stay here. I'll be right back."

Then she left. She was gone for a while. I used my time wisely. I snooped. I opened one of her filing cabinets and found a binder full of notes on all of the patients here. While reading and looking through the binder I found papers that were printed out. It was a fax that had been sent in not even five second before I walked through the door. It looked like this:

Name: Bree Larson
DOB: October, 17 1984
Status: In a relationship

Occupation: N/A

Reason for transfer: Emotional problems, fought with another patient over food, almost committed suicide after seeing her father in bed with another woman.

Yikes! I thought. Her dad cheated on her mom too. She was born three days before me. I bet she gets roomed with me. I heard footsteps and panicked. I threw the binder back into the cabinet and sat back in my seat and looked bored
.

The doctor came back with a camera and took pictures of my bruises. She promised my dad wouldn't get away with this ever again.

After meeting with her I had the rest of the day to myself. I just wanted to stay in my room and think. But of course I was interrupted. My test results were in.

"So what's the prognosis doc?" I asked.

"Well, see for yourself."

"You want me to read this?"

"Yes, out loud please."

"Patient Tiffany Carpenter has been diagnosed with…"

"Keep going."

"Has been diagnosed with Manic Depression and Bipolar disorder. You found all this out from a machine? What does this mean?"

"We found out from the machine and your session with your therapist. It means you'll be placed on medication. Starting tomorrow you will take your pills at breakfast and dinner everyday. Please try not to skip doses. We already informed your mother. We also have our staff on it."

"Wonderful."

On that note he turned around and left.

Day Two:

Woke up. Went to get my breakfast and there they were, the pills that I had to get used to. The ones for Bipolar Disorder were triangular and green and white. The ones for my Manic depression were really fat and huge and see-through red. They looked like Advil liqui gels only bigger. I swallowed them though.

Then off I go to an appointment. His name was Doctor Flemming. I went into his office where he questioned me just like Doctor Opitzki.

"The bruise on your face is quite a doozie."

"Yeah."

"Does it hurt?"

"Like I'm being hit repeatedly."

"And what about the ones on your sides?"

"Only when I breathe."

"Not if someone touches them?"

"DON'T TOUCH THEM!"

"I'm going to have a specialist come in and see you."

"Oh wonderful, and here I thought I wouldn't have to talk to any more doctors."

"Well you'll be talking to doctors until your last day, which is five days from now."

"So I get out of here in the morning on my seventh day?"

"Yes."

"What about my school?"

"We've notified them. You're not being marked absent except for the two days you were suspended which were today and yesterday. But tomorrow through Friday you're good.
Then you get out Sunday morning."

"Please tell me my dad isn't coming to get me."

"He isn't, your grandmother is."

"Yes! Thank goodness."

"Okay. You may go, time for dinner. Take those pills!"

"Yeah, yeah."

I ate, then I went to my room where I was surprised to find (we'll not really) Bree Larson.

"Hi," She said. "I'm your new roommate."

"Hey."

"You must be Tiff."

"You must be Bree."

"How did you know that? Doctor Opitzki said no one knew I was coming."

"About that."

"I'm listening."

"I went through her stuff."

"Wow," She laughed. "Looks like me and you have something in common. I would have done the same thing."

"My dad cheated on my mom too."

"How did you? Oh yeah. So then you know I almost killed myself."

"And that you fought some chick at the old place over a taco. Why?"

"Because that's what my dad made for the skank before I caught them in bed together."

"Ouch. I didn't really catch my dad. We just had a feeling we were right about. He cheated on her for seven years and once my mom found out she kicked him out, and he took his anger out on me as usual."

"Did he do that to you?"

"Yes."

"Do the Doctors here know?"

"Mhm."

"You know your dad's going to get it, right?"

"Serves him right."

Then sleep overcame me.

Day Three:

"Rise and shine Best Buddy!" Bree screamed.

"What?"

"It's time for breakfast!"

"Yay! Pill time."

"What?"

"They have me on pills for Bipolar Disorder and Manic Depression. Be careful when they send you to Doctor Lopaski."

"I go to him right after breakfast."

"Well, good luck with that. I'll see you back in the room."

"Bye."

I had no appointments until 6:00PM with my specialist. But I knew Bree would be walking through the door any second. I was right.

"Hey Best Buddy!" She said.

"Hi there."

"My results come at 5:00PM."

"That's in ten minutes."

"Yeah it is. Don't you have any appointments today?"

"Yeah at 6:00PM with some specialist for my bruises."

"Yowzah."

"Yup."

So we waited. I read and she wrote. Just then, Doctor Lopaski came in.

"What's up Doc?" I said.

"Who are you Bugs Bunny?"

"Sure."

"Anyway Bree here are your results please read them aloud."

She read, "Patient Bree Larson has been diagnosed with Manic Depression."

"You will be taking pills for the rest of your life." Doctor Lopaski replied.

"Do you say that to everyone? I asked.

"Very funny. I believe you have an appointment to get to? Bree you'll start…"

"Your treatment at breakfast tomorrow and dinner then continue it throughout your life." I said cutting him off.

"What she said."

"Bye!" We said in unison.

He left. I'm really getting sick of these Doctors now. Time rolled by 5:15, 5:30, 5:45 then 6:00.

"Time for my appointment." I said.

"Have fun!" Bree replied.

"Oh yeah, I'll have a blast."

"Haha."

"Bye."

Room A108 was where I was headed. I opened the door to find a familiar face. It was the Doctor that worked on me when my dad broke a few of my ribs way back when I was six.

"Doctor Shapinski?" I said questioningly.

"Hello Tiffany. Long time no see."

"Yeah ten years."

"So why don't you hop up on the table and we'll see what we're dealing with."

"Uh, okay."

I went up to the table while the Doctor examined my face. He looked at me with such concern. Then he touched my face and I yelped in pain and gritted my teeth. Then he had me lift my shirt and examined the bruises on my chest, back, and stomach. He touched the ones on my ribs and I screamed.

"Well we're going to need some X-rays." He said.

"Oh yay!"

"Sarcasm will get you nowhere."

"Actually, it will get me everywhere."

"Come over to room A109. We will take the X-ray's there."

"Okay, whatever you say."

We went into the next room and took the X-ray's and in no less than ten minutes they were ready.

"So what's wrong with me?"

"Well your cheek bone has been cracked."

"You mean broken?"

"Yes. Your jaw is dislocated."

"How can I talk then?"

"Complicated. You have four broken ribs."

"Wow Daddio. What a new record. I hope you're happy."

"Your dad deserves to be put away."

"Subject change! What are we going to do about my damages?"

"Your ribs I can take care of and your cheek I can fix in surgery, but your jaw will have to wait until tomorrow when I send in Doctor Martin. He specializes in that type of work."

"Okay. So when will we fix my cheek and ribs?"

"Tonight. Right now. In the emergency area."

"Double yay!"

"Come on, follow me."

I did. I couldn't risk defying any of them. That could mean more time in this dreadful place.

First, he put something over my ribcage and then wrapped me up with an ace bandage that went around my waist and shoulder. Then, he knocked me out. When I woke up I found out they put a metal plate in my cheek that covered the crack. Now I just have to worry about the stitches.

I spent the night in the emergency area.

Day Four:

I struggled to my feet. I got pushed in a wheelchair to breakfast to take my medicine. Then I was pushed back to room A108. There stood Doctor Martin all ready to get started.

Once again I was knocked out, not even knowing what they were going to do to my jaw. Then I woke up and saw myself. Headgear. Wonderful, just wonderful. My stitches don't come out for two weeks. My ribs don't heal for six-eight weeks. And the headgear doesn't come off for four-six weeks. School was going to be so much fun.

"Be careful with your ribs there isn't much we can do for them." Doctor Martin said.

"I will."

"Good."

"Why might I ask, is there a hospital in this place?"

"So the people who failed at suicide can be committed right away."

"Ah."

Day Five:

"Oh sleeping beauty." Bree said.

"What?"

"It's time for breakfast."

"Oh great, more people who can see me like this."

"Come on! It's not that bad."

"You're right. You know what? It's worse."

"You're still pretty."

"Oh, thanks."

"Come, come now. I'm hungry."

"But my whole face hurts. How am I supposed to eat?"

"I don't know. But you have to take your pills."

"You sound like my mother."

Then we left and just as I thought, I was laughed at. I was made fun of and whatsoever. All I did was take my pills. It was too much pain to bear. So I just sat at the table with Bree and waited for them to dismiss us.

"Why aren't you eating?" Bree asked.

"The same reason I'm barely talking."

"Oh yeah, your cheek and jaw. I keep forgetting."

"Just look at me. There's your reminder."

"So when are you leaving?

"In two days. You?"

"I have to wait a whole week yet."

"Well, that stinks."

"I know. Can I have your breakfast?"

"Take it."

"We need to exchange information before you go."

We stopped talking. I think she could tell I was in pain. I feel out of the loop. I miss Dante. Which reminded me I never asked about Bree's lover. I won't ask today. Afterall, I had an appointment in two hours.

I just wanted to get out already. It feels like I've been here forever. Sadly there is no escape.

Appointment time. Just wonderful. Today it's just me and Doctor Opitzki. So I walked in and shut the door behind me and sat down.

"Welcome Tiffany."

"Yeah."

"How do you feel?"

"Crappy."

"Are you in an extreme amount of pain?"

"Uh, yeah."

"Are you ready to leave this place?"

"Yes!"

"Well then I have good news for you."

"What?"

"Go pack your bags. You're going home."

"What? Why?"

"Let's just say good behavior."

"Thank you!"

"Your Grandma is waiting for you straight outside."

"Bye!"

I went to my room and told Bree the news. We were bummed but we exchanged info and I left. I went to the reception area and got my phone back. Then I went out and there my Grandma was. She said hi to me and then we were off. I turned on my cell phone to see if anyone called.

Nothing.

Nothing at all.

Not one call.

Not even a text message.

I was extremely angry and upset. I felt alone in the world. Like nobody cared about me at all. Dante didn't even text me. What kind of a boyfriend is that?

"So Tiff, how are you feeling?" My grandma asked.

"I feel like crap."

"What's the matter baby?"

The voice was coming from the backseat of the car. It was him, Dante.

"What are you doing here? I asked in astonishment.

"Did you think I was going to miss seeing you as soon as you got out?"

"How did you even know I was getting out today? I wasn't supposed to come out for another two days."

"I kept in touch with your mom."

"So how come you didn't text? You didn't even call."

"Because after you told me what happened with your dad and everything I contacted your mom and she told me everything."

"So you didn't even bother?"

"No."

"I guess I can understand that. So what do you think of my new look?"

"Why did you need it?"

"Cracked cheek, dislocated jaw."

"I'm going to kill your father."

"Then you'd both be in trouble!"

"I'm just so mad at him."

"He'll get what's coming to him. They promised me he'll get what's coming to him."

"Good."

"Now, if you don't mind, I'm going to take a nap."

We stopped talking. I couldn't sleep. The thought of my dad kept me awake. If he goes to prison, what happens when he gets out? Does he come after me? Does he vow for revenge? What happens at the court hearing? He'll lie. He'll tell them I'm bad on my own two feet. He'll say I'm a clutz. This is just too much to handle.

-Ring, Ring-

"Hello?" I said.

"Tiffany?" They answered.

"Yeah, who is this? The number is restricted."

"It's supposed to be."

"Why?"

"That's of little importance."

"What do you want from me?"

"To hear you scream in pain. You won't get away with this. I hope you know, I will find you."

"What did I do to you?"

"You opened your mouth. You ratted me out."

"Dad?"

-Click-

"Grandma?" I said hesitantly.

"What sweetheart?"

"I think that was my dad."

"What did he want?"

"Revenge, to hear me scream in pain."

"What!"

"That's what he said."

"Well, let's calm down. Give me your phone. I'm going to call your mother."

I gave her my phone and then punched the dashboard so hard I severed my knuckle. I was bleeding a lot.

"Now look at what you've done!" My grandma said.

"I'm sorry."

"Now we've got to take you to the hospital to get that fixed."

We drove to the nearest hospital. I got out and Dante followed, and my grandma went to find a parking place. I proceeded to go to the desk. I told the receptionist what happened and she gave me papers that I needed to fill out. I shouldn't have punched the dashboard. Look at what I have to do now because of it. I'm in yet another hospital.

The form I filled out was pretty simple and that was good. I didn't have the patience. I filled it out quickly and gave it back to the receptionist.

She took the forms and told me the Doctor would be right with me.

"Babe." Dante said.

"What?" I said hastily.

"Everything is going to be okay."

"How do you know? How could you possibly know that everything is going to be okay?"

"I can't explain it. It's just a feeling I have in the pit of my stomach. Just trust me."

"I do. I trust you."

"Uh- Miss Tiffany Carpenter?" The Doctor asked.

"That's me." I claimed.

"Goodness, what happened to you?" He asked.

"It's a long story."

"And we've got plenty of time."

So as we walked to the room we talked. I told him everything. Throughout the conversation I got a couple of "Oh dear!" and "Oh my God's!" He also asked about my hand. So I told him that story too.

"You're a mess!" He claimed.

"Got that right."

"He'll get what's coming to him."

"Let's hope so."

His name was Doctor Heart. Ironic I know. He was nice. It was only a matter of 30 minutes with the whole hand situation. He stitched up the gash in my knuckle and wrapped up my hand. I then went out to find my grandma and Dante waiting for me.

"How much do I owe you?" My Grandma asked the Doctor.

"Forget it." He exclaimed.

"Are you sure?" I asked.

"Don't worry about it. You've been through so much. Just forget it."

"Thank you." Me and my Grandma said.

We left. It took us a while to find the car. About 20 minutes later we found it, once again on our journey back home.

I spent the drive thinking I was going insane. I really am a mess. I can't believe how in the matter of a year my whole world crashed and plummeted to the ground. Leaving me with scars. Literally. I'm starting to think that life isn't even worth it anymore.

"What's the point?" I said finally.

"What are you talking about sweetie?" My Grandma replied.

"What's the point?"

"Honey, what are you getting at?"

"I need to know, grandma. I need to know."

"Know what?"

"What the point is!"

"You're not making any sense!"

"Really?"

PART FOUR

We were on the freeway. We were going about 70mph. I was going to do it.

My life flashed before my eyes.

I undid my seatbelt, opened the door and there I went. Down the embankment rolling, tumbling, then darkness. Nothingness.

When I woke up, I was in a hospital bed. No one around me. There was an I.V. in my arm. And a cast around my leg. The rest of me was scrapes and bruises, and what was once just an ace bandage on my wrist was now a cast. I then felt a sharp pain in my side and I looked to see that I was bleeding.

"Ow!" I screamed in pain. I started shaking uncontrollably. I pushed the call button for the nurses.

Then once again, NOTHING. Darkness. All I heard was frantic beeping but then in a matter of seconds it faded. Nothing. I was in and out for hours. One hour I'm surrounded by doctors, the next I'm asleep.

All I felt was pain. My failed attempt at suicide did nothing. It only worsened the cause.

When I was finally up and alert. I noticed someone holding my hand beside me. Which was unusual. I was in Intensive Care. Why would they let anyone in here? I reached for my glasses and put them on my face. I glanced over. It was him. It was my Father.

"Help!" I screamed, frantically pushing the call button. "Help!" I shouted again.

A nurse ran through my door. I started bleeding again.

"Get him out of here! Get him out!" I shouted.

More doctors burst through the door. Everyone in a frenzy.

"Make him go." I cried. "Please make him go!"

"Sir, I'm going to have to ask you to leave." One Doctor exclaimed.

"I'm not going anywhere." My dad screamed.

"Make him go! Make him go!" I screamed once more.

"Sir, I'm only going to ask you one more time. Please leave." Said the Doctor.

"I SAID NO!" My father screamed.

One nurse ran out of the room then soon came back with security. My father laughed incessantly and lunged at me. Only to be counter attacked by the officer. He pinned my father down. I was crying. Doctors and nurses surrounded me from all sides.

"What's the matter?" One asked.

"I-I don't ever want him in here again." I wept, "Never do you understand?"

"Okay" They replied, asking no questions.

I cried myself to sleep. I slept for only about 20 minutes. I was awakened by a Doctor changing the I.V. in my arm.

"I'm sorry I awakened you." He exclaimed.

"It's okay." I mumbled.

"Why can't that man come here?"

"Because he's the reason for all of this. This whole mess!"

"What do you mean?"

"He abused me. My whole life! I wanted to rid myself of it."

"I understand. We will keep him out. I promise."

"Good. Can I ask you something?"

"Yes"

"What is wrong with me? Exactly."

"Well you broke your leg and your arm. You also broke three ribs on the left side of your body. Plus, I know you can't see it but you have a gash about 7 inches long on your back."

"Wow. What about this?" I asked, pointing to my side where I kept continually bleeding.

"That my dear is where we had to remove your appendix."

"What? Why?"

"Well, when you jumped out of the car and tumbled down the hill a sharp piece of rock broke off inside of you. It lodged into your appendix and caused it to rupture."

"God, I really am a mess."

"You need some rest."

I slowly drifted to sleep. The doctor gave me something to help me sleep more soundly. I appreciated it. I needed it!

When I awoke from my peaceful slumber, I slowly turned over to my side and noticed another figure. I was wearily and hesitatingly reaching for my glasses. I slowly put them on my face and looked over. It was him. Dante. He was once again here for me in my most unstable of conditions.

"You seem to be popping up everywhere!" I joked.

"You're awake!" He replied while turning around.

"Yeah. How long have you been here?"

"I've been here a while."

"That doesn't necessarily answer my question."

"For hours."

"What? Why'd you stay so long?"

"I wanted to see you. I had to make sure you were okay."

"Oh."

"Why did you do it?"

"Why?"

"Yes! Why? Tiffany! Why?"

"Listen, I don't need your tone! I'm in a hospital for crying out loud! I'm in a whole lot of pain! I don't need this on top of everything."

"Look, I'm sorry. It's just that my psycho girlfriend just plummeted down a hill trying to kill herself. Forgive me for being a little upset!"

"I thought you said I wasn't a mess! I thought you said I was just misunderstood!"

"Well maybe I was wrong!"

"You know what? Maybe this is wrong!"

"Ow" I screamed. I looked down and I was bleeding. "You see? You see what you do? You get my blood going because my heart is racing."

"So now it's all my fault?"

"Yes! Now go! And don't come back!

It's over!"

"Tiff-"

"No! Leave!"

And that's exactly what he did. He left the side of my bed and stopped at the door. Then there was that awkward moment. You know, the moment after a break up where one or the both of you has something to say but nothing can come out. That was the moment we were having. There he was just standing at the door in the middle of the doorway, the both of us just looking at each other. Then when I couldn't take It anymore I turned facing the other direction showing no remorse. No sign of sadness. No sign of regret.

I heard him leave. Me a mess? Maybe! Insane though? He crossed the line. Why now? I just have to ask. As if things couldn't get any worse. I wasted the day away begging Doctors to call my Doctors from the mental institute.

They did just so. Dr. Lopaski was going to come and see me tomorrow. That calmed my nerves a little bit.

Throughout the day and throughout the night I got close with the doctors. I
had a different doctor or nurse come in every few hours. I made them bring me movies with them and I demanded that they stay with me because I couldn't be alone. I just couldn't stand the silence. I stayed up all night with a nurse named Anne. She was nice. She was the only person at this place who hasn't gotten tired of me yet. It turns out that I've been here for a week. When I thought it was only for 2 days.

I guess I was out longer than I thought. This year just hadn't been what I wanted, what I expected. Now I'm certifiably insane. I'm single. And I'm banged up pretty good. Literally I'm a mess. I cried my-self to sleep that night.

I felt miserable. I have so much that is going wrong in my life. So many issues and I get rid of the only thing that's going right. I am worthless.

"Tiffany, sweetheart? wake up" I heard a voice say.

I opened my eyes to see Anne standing there with Dr. Lopaski.

"Um...hi" I managed to say.

"How are you?" He asked.

"Feeling the pain. Too much pain."

"Physical? Emotional?"

"Both"

"You wanna talk about it?"

"Well yeah! That's kinda why I asked them to call you down."

"So do you want me to ask questions, or do you just wanna talk?"

"Questions first, then we'll see if I wanna talk later."

"Ok. So why'd you do it?"

"Do what? I've done a lot of stupid things!"

"Why did you jump out of the car?"

"Impulse!"

"What do you mean?"

"I acted on an impulse. I just wanted to die."

"Why?"

"Well... my Father called. Just as soon as I got out, he called."

"What did he want?"

"To hear me scream in pain. He wanted revenge! But I didn't do anything wrong!" I screamed, crying.

"Don't work yourself up. You will only make it worse. He will not hurt you."

I spoke through my teeth, "How do you know?"

"We're going to get you help."

"Ha!" I laughed, almost sounding insane. "Help? What are you guys gonna do to help? I think I'm a little past the brink of help! You tried to help me all that did was prove I was insane. And even the medication didn't help! I jumped out of a car for crying out loud!"

"You are not insane."

I laughed.

"We cannot help the fact that you jumped out of a car. But we can still help you!"

"I don't see how!" I muttered.

"I will come back here everyday if I have to. Just for you to see that there is still hope. I will not have you giving up again. You don't need to fear anything. We will help you. We will make things okay."

"I have a very hard time trusting that concept. EVERYTHING WILL BE OKAY! HA! That would be a nice change of pace. Having nothing to worry about."

That's when I almost lost it. I started shaking uncontrollably. Dr. Lopaski's eyes went wide like he never saw anything like that before.

"I need a doctor!" I screamed.

He ran out of the room and came in with two doctors. "What's going on with her?" I heard someone say.

"I don't know, she just started shaking. She asked me to run and get you" Dr. Lopaski replied.

Then darkness. Once again I was out.

I woke up to a room filled with eyes, all of them of course on me. My mom was there, along with Virg and the twins. My Grandma was there too. They all stared at me, eyes flickering across my body. Probably wondering why I did what I did. I closed my eyes and said, "You were right, Mom!"

There was a gasp, quickly followed by screams from the twins, "She's awake! Tiffs awake!"

I smiled. I hadn't realized how much I really missed my family.

"What was I right about, baby?" My Mom answered.

"Um...how about everything."

"Like? Be more specific honey."

"How much of a mess I truly am."

"Honey...I-I should have never sent you away. Especially with your father. I-I'm so sorry. I didn't realize...I'm so sorry."

"Mom. Stop. This isn't your fault. You didn't do anything. You set me on the right track my whole life! You didn't knock me off of it, I did. And it's up to me to get myself back on track."

"Tiffany sweetie, You've grown so much."

"Well when you're forced to it really isn't all that hard."

"But still I shouldn't have sent you with your father. Of all people."

"Mom, it's okay. I'm okay."

"Look at you. You're always trying to be so strong."

"I am strong."

"Yeah but even strong people can crumble."

"Yep. And I reached my breaking point."

"Why did you jump out of that car?"

"Dad called me."

"Ah! You don't have to go any further if you don't want to."

"No. It's okay."

"Are you sure?"

"Yes."

"Okay."

"Well it started out like a normal conversation the number was restricted though. So I asked who it was and they claimed it was of little importance. So I asked what they wanted. Then that's when all the pieces fit together."

I started shaking again. I want to know why does this keep happening to me? The memory I tried to suppress? My Father? Was he the route of my insanity? Am I crazy?!? I drifted again.

I should be a rock. Lifeless. Without feeling.

I woke up to just my mom. She was holding my hand crying. I can't believe she thinks this is all her fault! How could she? Why would she? Poor Mom.

"I love you Mom" I spoke.

"I love you too"

"I don't want you to think this is all your fault." I said touching her face.

She kept my hand there with hers and spoke softly, "It was just the fact that me and your dad, I should have taken you myself."

"Mom, you can't change the past. But we can change our future. Dad will get his, and I'll heal. Just don't blame yourself or I'll be highly upset."

"I'll try to be strong for you, my little rock."

I smiled. Ha a rock. If only, if only. I wish.

"Mom?" I spoke.

"What is it?"

"I don't wanna be rude but I'd really like to be alone for a while. I need to think."

"It's okay I'll come back first thing tomorrow morning. I love you."

"I love you too."

And so she left. I was ALONE.

I wanted to clear my head. I wanted to write. That's exactly what I did. It might have been sloppy but my knuckle is broken. Along with many other things. I just wanted to let my feelings flow. This is what I wrote:

Ignorant fool.

Insult being.

Letting feelings get in the way.

Stupid feelings.

Restless pain.

Stupid ignorant fool.

Stupid insulant being.

And then for the first time in weeks. I cried. I cried like I've never cried before. You could say I was hysterical. Borderline insanity. So much to bear. TOO MUCH. I hate this. I hate him. My father. Yeah, thanks a lot daddy. This is all his fault. I did not deserve any of his crap.

I stayed crying. Then Anne, my friend, came into the room.

"Hi," She said.

"Hey."

"You were crying an awful lot. Are you in pain?"

"Yes."

"Do you need something?"

"Completely."

"I'll stay as long as you wish."

"Thanks."

We talked for hours. We watched movies. And we laughed. It hurt me a little but I was feeling better. It got late though and she had to bid me farewell.

As soon as she left though, to my surprise, I fell asleep. For the first time on my own. Not with one of my "fits" as I call them. I didn't know how truly exhausted I was. But sleep felt good.

I woke up to a strange figure standing in the corner of my room staring out the window. It was obvious that it was a guy so I tensed.

"Who is it?" I screamed.

"Tiffany..." the voice trailed off. I realized who it was.

"What do you want, James?"

"Forgiveness, another..."

"Chance?" I cut him off.

"Yes"

"Things didn't work out with Keana?"

"No. She wasn't you."

"What do I look like to you James, a rebound? Do I look stupid? I fell for this line of bull once I won't do it again."

"Tiffany I'm so sorry."

"That just doesn't quite cut it anymore."

"What will then? Come on baby I'm on my knees. I love you!"

"Ha. You love me? You're insane."

"No I'm not. I love you. I truly do. You mean so much to me. You just, you have no idea."

"I know you think you love me. I believe that. But you don't know what love is. If I say yes...again. Foolishly. I know what will happen. You'll take me, then you'll break me and leave me with the pieces. But I have enough to put back together. I don't need anything else broken."

"Tiffany, listen. You are the best thing that ever happened to me. I was a fool to let you slip through my fingers. The truth is I was afraid."

"What were you afraid of?"

"Losing you. And this, the accident. It shook me. It made me realize what's important in my life."

"Well maybe you should have thought about that before you cheated on me."

"I'm sorry I was afraid I acted out. It meant nothing. Me and Keana didn't even last."

"Is that supposed to make me feel any better?"

"I don't know. All I know is that I do love you."

"No you don't. Listen, I do not want to be bothered with this now. I want to be alone."

"Okay. I'll go."

"Bye."

He left. That was easier than I thought. He gave me no grief. Why me? Why'd he have to come back to me? He doesn't love me. He just wants me back because he thinks I'm stupid. That I'll bend to his every whim, but I'm stronger than that. Better than that.

I am a mindless pool of confusion waiting for things to change, to get better. Life as I knew it was over as soon as my father stepped into the picture after all these years. I was finally having a little bit of peace. Finally finding me. I guess it's true how one bad thing can really mess you up. My life has become the complete opposite of what I wanted it to be.

How could this possibly have happened to me? I am a good person. I always try to be nice to people. Yet, people walk all over me, and they take advantage of me. James. The nerve of him. Coming back. Showing up at the hospital. I swear he is the only person in the world who could drive me so crazy! So what does that mean? Does it mean that I'm just angry? Was dating Dante just revenge? How messed up does that sound? I did care about Dante. He is sweet. I did care for James too. James was my best friend. I loved James,

I really, really loved him. But could I ever trust him again? The truth is I'd take him back in a heartbeat. But does that make me weak? I am so mad at him. Once a cheater, always a cheater, right? Maybe not. But what about Dante? My Dante. He'll be so pissed. He is the safe choice, perhaps. I don't want to be safe. Maybe I want passion. Maybe I want to love so much it hurts. I've made up my mind. I made my choice.

I reached for the nurse call button and pushed it. Anne came through the door. My wonderful friend Anne.

"You rang?" she asked.

"Yes"

"What can I help you with? Are you in pain?"

"Well, yes. But that's not what I wanted you for."

"Okay. I'll send you something for your pain. What did you want then?"

"The guy, the one who was just in here."

"Yes. I saw him."

"Is he still here?"

"I'll go see while I get you something for your pain."

"Thank you."

She left. She was quick. In a flash she was back and putting who knows what in my I.V.

"I didn't see him in the waiting room, Hun." She said.

"Oh. Okay. Thanks."

"Anything else?"

"No."

She left. I was all alone again.

The silence is killer. It gives me far too much time to think, to reflect. That's never good in my case. My whole life has been a series of "should I do this?" which always ended in the same way. I do what I want. Then I face the outcome head on. Whatever the outcome may be. And as I lay there thinking and reflecting, I drifted into sleep.

I woke up, not even thirty minutes later. I had a bad dream. He was in it. My Father. Sleep would be completely impossible for the remainder of the night. So I turned on the television and I watched movies till morning.

I heard a knock on the door at around 7:30am. It was my mom, back in the morning just like she said she'd be. Good ol' Mom.

"Hey sweetie." She said.

"Hi, Mom."

"How are you feeling?"

"Conflicted, and sore."

"Do you want me to see if they can do anything for your pain?"

"What I want is this thing off of my head already."

"Your headgear? Are you sure? You look cute."

"Shut up, Mom," I laughed. "I want it off."

"I can ask about that later. First, tell me why you're conflicted."

"Mom?"

"Yes?"

"If dad only cheated on you one time and wasn't so violent, could you have found it in your heart to forgive him?"

"Where is this coming from?"

"Can you just answer the question?"

"I loved your father very much, Tiffany. He was my best friend. If it was only once, I would have taken him back in a second. If people said I was foolish, I wouldn't have cared."

"Wow."

"The heart wants what the heart wants Tiff, if your heart is talking to you, don't ignore it."

"Thanks Mom."

"Sure sweetie."

"Could you get me some food please?"

"Be right back."

She left. I love the heart to hearts I have with my mom. She has always been so loving and supportive. My whole life it's always been that way.

My Mom wasn't gone for long. She brought me back salmon and veggies. My favorite. As I ate, my Mom just watched me, smiling. She was probably thinking, "Thank God, my daughter is still alive." I think seeing her like that is what made me stop hurting myself.

A few months went by of me going through therapy and just getting better all together. They were very long months where I didn't really talk to anyone. I kept to myself and my family. I could walk again without crutches. I could make a fist again. It was progress. My dad was in prison, with no chance of early parole. I was single. I didn't want to make any hasty decisions, not right then anyway. Did I mention I was driving? A beautiful Oldsmobile Cutlass Siera, white.

I was also seventeen, maturing.

I was headed to the grocery store. My mother needed things and she was taking advantage of my new four wheels. I pulled out of the driveway and went. I loved driving. It was...relaxing. The store isn't that far from us, I could have walked, I just didn't want to. I pulled in the spot, and pulled out the shopping list:

-eggs

-milk

-toilet paper

-dish soap

-salmon

-chicken

-frozen pizza's (the twins fav.)

-iced tea (no more soda)

-potatoes

-carrots

-celery

Love, Mom

Oh, my Mom. She's a riot. I love her.

Aisle 1. That's where the eggs and milk are located. That's where I went first and that's where I saw him. Dante. It had to have been six months since I saw him last. Since the hospital.

He hadn't changed much, not in the least. When I noticed he wasn't alone, I had to admit it stung a little. Just a little. Then I noticed her, and that's when she noticed me.

"Tiff!" She shouted.

"Keana."

"Dante! Look who's here!" She shouted.

"Hi, Tiffany." He said.

"Hello." I replied.

"Dante and I got back together!" She stated.

"That's just wonderful." I said.

"Are you still crazy?" Keana exclaimed.

"Are you still a whore?" I replied.

"Stop it, you two." Dante interrupted.

"No, I'm not crazy. It's called a disorder and I'm on medication. I sure hope you've stopped cheating though, because he deserves better than that. Now if you'll excuse me." I shoved my cart right through them.

The nerve she had calling me crazy. I made some bad choices, but that doesn't make me crazy. I hated her. I couldn't believe Dante took her back. She just doesn't like me because we fought. That was on her though. Whore. Dante must have had a lot of love for her in his heart if he took her back. Or, maybe she changed. Maybe he just forgave. Maybe that's what I needed to do.

I grabbed the rest of my groceries and checked out. I didn't want to risk bumping into them again. I parked in the driveway and put everything where it belonged.

After I finished I ran up to my room and just sat there and I wrote :

Time seems to fly

Faster then the rain falls from the sky

Faster then the tears fall from my eyes

Every glance

Is another moment wasted

Letting go is a choice

Moving forward is a must.

I let myself get caught up in my mind.

I didn't go to school anymore. I graduated early, well, I got my GED. School wasn't an option in my condition. I didn't want to be bothered. I spent my days writing a lot and spending time with my grandma. Life was simple and simple was nice.

Later, I took a shower. I had to wash my day away. I wanted to go out. I hadn't been out in awhile. I didn't have any friends anymore though. It kind of ruled the idea of going out, out. That's when I decided that I needed a friend. Any kind of friend would do.

After my shower I went to my computer. "Time to research." I said aloud. So I typed "puppies for free" in my google search bar. To my surprise there were a lot of people who had little pups that just couldn't afford to take care of them. That was when I saw her. The cutest little puppy you could ever imagine, I contacted the owners right away. I could get her the following day, they said. I was excited.

I went to bed. Sleep was welcomed by my happiness. Morning came before I knew it. It was going to be a good day. That I knew for a fact.

I got up and got dressed. I walked to my brother's room, I was curious as to if they wanted to come with me.

"Hey Virg?" I knocked.

"What's up, Tiff?"

"I'm going out. Do you want to come?"

"No, I'm hanging out with some friends."

"That's ok! I'll see you later, have fun!"

I couldn't wait anymore. I was far too excited. So I grabbed my keys and I left. As I was driving I thought of names. Tinker, Onyx, Choco...I couldn't decide.

Before I knew it, I was there. I walked to the door and rang the doorbell.

"Hello." A woman answered.

"Hi, I'm Tiffany. I called yesterday about the dogs."

"Oh yes! Right this way."

She led me through the living room and past the kitchen to this tiny closet off the side. There they were. So cute, so playful.

"There are three boys and five girls. Take as many as you want. They deserve a good home." She said.

I sat on the floor and played with them. There were two of them that were especially friendly to me. A little boy and a little girl.

"I'll take these two." I said to her.

"Alright, thank you so much. They deserve a good, happy home."

"Thank you!"

She showed me the way out. I put them right on my passenger seat.

They were little pugs. Too cute. A boy and a girl! The boy's name was Max, and the girl's name was Tinny. I drove straight to the pet store. I needed collars, leashes, and name tags. Oh, the excitement! In my opinion dogs make everything better. They're far better than people, that's for sure.

PART FIVE

Another year flew by with its own twists and turns. I even got married, can you believe it? His name is Joshua. He was so sweet and so cute, he even wrote me poems. I allowed myself to fall into this blissful ignorance. I allowed him to take over my life, my thoughts, you name it.

After a year we got pregnant. I was excited, I always wanted to be a mom. Sadly, though, I ended up miscarrying. It was devastating. It made me think that my body was broken.

I went through so many unfriendly and unpleasant thoughts. I hated myself. I really did, it was an awful time and Joshua never got it, he always would tell me "it's not real, if you did it was only cells."

Am I the only one who believes that life happens at conception? There wouldn't be any cells if the sperm and eggs didn't fuse together.

"All living things are made up of cells you know." I'd often reply.

And you know what? If it wasn't real for him, it was very real to me. Two more years had passed before I got pregnant again.

The pregnancy for the most part went smoothly. I got sick but it only lasted for 2 weeks.

When I hit 20 weeks pregnant I started to bleed. I was petrified. I couldn't lose another baby, not this far along. I went to the hospital so scared. I was hooked up to so many monitors. Thankfully everything was okay.

My pregnancy continued on pretty normally after that, except for the fact that I got huge and retained so much water. You could literally poke my leg and it would leave an indentation in my leg. Crazy right?

Labor was another story. I lasted 37 and 1/2 hours. Yup. You read that correctly. 37 1/2. My water broke before I started any contractions so they had to start them themselves. When I was finally dilated to 10cm and pushing for 2.5 hours, they made the decision to take me to the O.R and gave me a C-Section.

I felt them slice me open. It was horrific. But within a few moments my sweet baby boy was on my chest, and NOTHING else mattered. Taking care of that sweet baby was all I wanted to do. Joshua and I decided to name him Noah, and Noah was perfect.

His sugars were low though so he had to go to the NICU. My sweet boy spent the first 24 hours of his life away from me. I think that messed with my mentality too. We spent 5 days in the hospital.

Another year passed and I was pregnant again, this pregnancy was far from smooth. I was sick every single day of those 37 weeks. It was awful. And the beginning I was spotting and so dehydrated I swear I spent the first few months in and out of the hospital. I had a repeat C-Section with him too. The surgery and recovery went so much smoother this time around. We named him Eric.

He had some breathing issues but his NICU stay helped get him back on the right track. This time around I also stayed 5 days in the hospital.

Adjusting to life with two kids was far from easy. Yet, what did we do? Got pregnant again. This time around it started off just like Eric's pregnancy, rough.

I was sick everyday and spotting for weeks. Then about a week from my 21 week anatomy scan I developed a pain in my side that wasn't unbearable, but just enough to be annoying. So I went to the Doctor to be safe.

They did an ultrasound and checked her heart rate (yup, finally a girl) . It was 170bpm and when she pushed down on my belly it didn't hurt so they sent me home.

"Whew! my baby is okay" I thought to myself.

So I went home, took Tylenol like she told me to.

Fast forward to my anatomy scan. She was literally on my belly for two seconds, before I got the worst news of my life (so far).

"There is no heartbeat." She said it was so cold and callous.

"What do you mean?" I replied.

"Your baby has no heartbeat."

At that moment I broke. I cried and cried and they made me leave out the back way. As if they didn't want me to worry the other moms with "healthy pregnancies" day.

I had to go to the hospital and deliver her. This labor was the worst. I had nothing for my pain. And to make matters worse, I wound up giving birth to her in the toilet. I still can't pee without having a flashback to that moment.

I was clotting something fierce after her birth. They had to give me a shot of something in my hip to help control it. They proceeded to go inside of me arms deep and physically pull the clots out. It hurt so bad without pain medication.

After they cleaned her up I got to hold her. My sweet little Kehlani. She was so small and so perfectly formed. She was a little bigger than my hand if you needed a visual.

I kept her for 11 hours kissing her, cuddling her, and saying my goodbyes. I didn't want to give her up, but her looks were changing and her face was caving in and I didn't want anything to interfere with her autopsy.

I needed answers. I needed to know why this happened. I did everything right. I was on top of every pain and concern with my doctors. So why? Why did my baby have to die? I internalized it and blamed myself.

We never got an answer. I think that's what messes with me too, the uncertainty.

PART SIX

Fast forward to now. Now I'm writing this as a single mom of two boys whose husband left her two weeks to the day of their daughters passing, because he was cheating.

"Losing her made me realize I didn't want to try anymore." He'd say.

"What do you mean? I didn't even know we had a problem."

I literally begged him for my chance, as if I was in the wrong. I cried to him, "not now, why now?" a million times. But why would someone even give a chance when they're already in a whole new relationship.

Can you imagine being so broken from just losing your sweet baby to then have to go through the grief of losing your marriage? How just one of those events alone would be enough to break a person. Yet, here I am. Struggling every moment.

Here I am now a single mom thrown back into the working world. Struggling, but doing it because my kids inspire the "greatness" that is buried in me. They only deserve the very best.

Living with a disability doesn't make me incapable. It may mess with my head and cause me more anxiety than you'll ever know but I'm am determined to persevere. For my kids, for my Kehlani.

Where is life going to take me from here? I guess we'll just have to wait and see.

THE END

...or is it?

Made in the USA
Middletown, DE
29 April 2022

64993253R00046